by **Patricia Reilly Giff**

pictures by **Laura J. Bryant**

Orchard Books • New York • An Imprint of Scholastic Inc.

"I have my own new room,"

I told Bella the babysitter.

"A new bed, too. It's gigantic!"

Bella jangled her bracelets.

"Time for a new-room present, Patti Cake.

I'll take you shopping tomorrow."

I couldn't wait.

That night, the room turned greatly dark.
No one slept in that big bed but me.
Even Tootsie slept in the hall.

The next morning, I put on my light-up ring and my cowgirl hat with the strings.
We were off to Mr. Herman's Everything Store.

I galloped up one aisle and down another.

We went to the aisle with the dolls.
I opened a box. Yes!

The doll inside had frizzly hair
and blush on one cheek.
"Are you alone in the greatly dark?" I asked.
Poor doll. I knew how she felt.

"This doll's on sale," said Bella the babysitter.
"She's a little smudgy, too."
Sometimes I get a little smudgy.
Besides, I loved her name. On-Sale.
It was a two-word name like mine. Patti Cake.
"No more dark box for you," I told her.

At home, we marched into the bathroom.

"Time to get un-smudged," I said.

On-Sale was shy without her sparkly dress.

And she wasn't happy with her gray cloth body

that didn't even have a belly button.

I found my nail polish.

In two minutes, On-Sale had

a lovely pink belly button.

So did the sink, the floor, and the shower sheet.

"Get ready to be un-smudged," I told On-Sale.

I blasted on the water.

Tootsie blasted out of the tub.

Why was she taking a nap in there anyway?

Tootsie ran over the nail polish.

She ran over On-Sale.

Now On-Sale had five belly buttons.

Tootsie raced out the door like a wild buffalo.

On-Sale was afraid.

She wasn't used to stampeding dogs
and bathtubs with blasting water.

"Don't worry," I said.
"You don't have to get into the tub.
You can get un-smudged right here on the floor."

"Patti Cake," called Bella. "Let's have a new-room party!"

She baked a pink whooshly cake.

She cut a piece for me and one for On-Sale.

Tootsie jumped on the table.

She loved cake.

She took a chunk from the top.

"Down!" yelled Bella.

I helped On-Sale with her cake.

Oh, no!

Tootsie ate On-Sale's cake.
Then she grabbed On-Sale.
I raced after them.
Oops, there went the cake
in a pink whooshly pile on the floor.
"Hold on, On-Sale," I yelled.

We landed in a heap.
Tootsie was gobbling up the cake.
I hoped she wouldn't gobble up
On-Sale.

Tootsie hid behind the couch.
We could just see her tail.

"You're out of danger now," I told On-Sale.
"Tomorrow, we'll un-smudge you again."

At bedtime, On-Sale and I were ready to sleep in the greatly dark together.

I put her sparkly dress on the bottom of the bed.
It was sweet and sticky.
So was her face.
I turned off the light.
We climbed in.
But then —

In came Tootsie.
She jumped up on the bed.
She licked On-Sale's sticky face.
"She is saying she's sorry," I said.
"She wants to be your friend."

I gave Tootsie a pat.

She stretched out.

She went to sleep on On-Sale's dress.

A light came into the window.

I could see On-Sale.

I could see Tootsie.

I could see my new room.

It wasn't greatly dark anymore.

It was just . . .

great.

Love to my own Patti Cake O'Meara — P.R.G.

For my sweetie-pie — L.J.B.

Text copyright © 2014 by Patricia Reilly Giff • Illustrations copyright © 2014 by Laura J. Bryant • All rights reserved. Published by Orchard Books, an imprint of Scholastic Inc., *Publishers since 1920.* ORCHARD BOOKS and design are registered trademarks of Watts Publishing Group, Ltd., used under license. SCHOLASTIC and associated logos are trademarks and/or registered trademarks of Scholastic Inc. • No part of this publication may be reproduced, stored in a retrieval system, or transmitted in any form or by any means, electronic, mechanical, photocopying, recording, or otherwise, without written permission of the publisher. For information regarding permission, write to Orchard Books, Scholastic Inc., Permissions Department, 557 Broadway, New York, NY 10012. • Library of Congress Cataloging-in-Publication Data • Giff, Patricia Reilly. • Patti Cake and her new doll / by Patricia Reilly Giff; illustrated by Laura J. Bryant. — 1st ed. • p. cm.   Summary: Patti Cake is a little girl with a brand new big girl room and a new, but slightly smudged, doll to keep her company — if her dog, Tootsie, does not run away with it. • ISBN 978-0-545-24465-7 (hardcover: alk. paper) 1. Dolls — Juvenile fiction. 2. Dogs — Juvenile fiction. [1. Dolls — Fiction. 2. Dogs — Fiction. 3. Humorous stories.] I. Bryant, Laura J., ill. II. Title. • PZ7.G3626Pat 2013 • 813.54 — dc23 • 2012015712 • 10 9 8 7 6 5 4 3 2 1   14 15 16 17 18 • Printed in China   38 • Reinforced Binding for Library Use • First edition, January 2014 • The display type was set in Chaloops Bold. • The text was set in Kuenstler 480 BT. • Laura J. Bryant created her illustrations with watercolor paint and colored pencil on smooth Bristol board. • Book design by Chelsea C. Donaldson